Rabbit
and
Coyote

by Susan McCloskey   illustrated by Leovigileo Martínez

Scott Foresman

Editorial Offices: Glenview, Illinois • New York, New York
Sales Offices: Reading, Massachusetts • Duluth, Georgia
Glenview, Illinois • Carrollton, Texas • Menlo Park, California

This is a story from Mexico my mother told me. She heard it from her parents, who came to this country as immigrants soon after they married. They worked very hard, and they had two children. (One of them, my mother, is now an engineer. The other, my uncle, is a teacher.) My grandparents told the story to their children, who told it to their children. And I will tell it to mine.

Like my grandparents, the immigrants, this story has traveled far from its home. Who knows where it started or where it will travel next?

Now, when people in this country look at the full moon, they see the face of a man. "The Man in the Moon," they call him. But when people in Mexico look at the same moon, they see a rabbit. I will tell you how the rabbit got on the moon.

One night the moon shone down on a field of chili peppers. And in that field of chilies was Rabbit, eating the biggest and juiciest ones.

"*¡Qué delicioso!*—How delicious!" Rabbit said as he munched. "Surely Bear grows the best chilies in all of Mexico!"

Bear was very angry when he saw that someone had been eating his chilies. He was determined to catch the thief. So he decided to set a trap. He made a bear out of beeswax, which is very soft and sticky. He put the beeswax bear right beside a plant loaded with plump chilies.

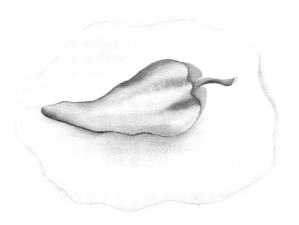

That evening Rabbit returned to the field to get some more chilies for his supper.

"Good evening, Bear," he said politely to the beeswax bear. "Do you mind sharing some of your fine chilies with me?"

The bear didn't say anything. Rabbit said some other nice things to the bear as well. But no matter what he said, or how often he said it, the beeswax bear stood there. It was as silent as a stone.

Rabbit got very angry at the bear's rudeness.

"Bear, I hate to say this, but your mother has taught you no manners. Or do you think you are too important to speak to me?" he asked, pushing the bear's chest. His paw stuck fast.

¡Ay! ¡Qué sorpresa! What a surprise!

Rabbit had not expected this. He pushed the bear with his other paw, then with his two back feet. In no time at all, Rabbit was so stuck that he could hardly twitch his nose.

In the morning Bear went to his field. When he saw Rabbit, he said, "What a fine big rabbit you are! And what a wonderful meal you will make!"

Bear put Rabbit in a sack and carried him home over his shoulder. There he set a pot of water on to boil, throwing in some chilies and some potatoes. Then he went to tell his wife and children to get ready for a feast.

While Bear was gone, Coyote came by.

As soon as Rabbit saw him, he got an idea. Before Coyote could say a word, Rabbit spoke up.

"Coyote, you're invited to a feast! Look, Bear and I have chilies and potatoes cooking in the pot. I am keeping the bread inside this sack warm. Why don't you take my place so I can go home to get my guitar. Then we will have good music as well as good food!"

Coyote gladly did as Rabbit suggested. He let Rabbit out of the sack and climbed in to take his place.

Bear soon returned. When he saw that
Rabbit was gone, he was very angry.

"Coyote, you put your nose where it
doesn't belong! I will teach you to mind your
own business!" he said. Then he flung Coyote
into the pot of hot water.

As you can imagine, Coyote jumped out of
that pot like a shot. He ran off, very wet and
very angry. He vowed not to rest until he
found Rabbit.

Soon Coyote came to a hill. On the hill was a rock. And leaning against the rock was Rabbit.

"I've got you now!" Coyote said.

But Rabbit said, "Oh, I'm not going anywhere. Can't you see that if I don't hold back this rock, it will roll down the hill and crush the villagers? Here! You take my place while I go for help."

Coyote wondered if Rabbit was trying to fool him again. But then Rabbit said, "Hurry! There's no time to wait!"

So again Coyote took Rabbit's place.

It didn't take Coyote long to realize that Rabbit had tricked him again. Off he went, looking for Rabbit. He looked and looked until the sun sank from the sky.

Now the full moon made the night almost as bright as day. So Coyote had no trouble seeing Rabbit sitting on the shore of a lake.

"Hello, Coyote," said Rabbit as the angry Coyote approached him. "I'm so sorry I made you angry! Let me make it up to you."

"Let's forget the past and be friends," Rabbit went on. "I just collected a little bit of honey. I will share it with you."

Coyote still had his doubts. But he was hungry. And the honey looked delicious! So he sat down to eat with Rabbit.

In fact, the honey was so delicious that Coyote ate almost all of it. Then he felt bad that he had taken most of Rabbit's honey.

"Don't worry," said Rabbit. "There's more honey right there in the hole in that tree. Just reach in and get a full jar for us. There's nothing to it!"

Now Coyote had never collected honey
before. So he just grabbed the jar and dunked
it deep into the hole in the tree. He filled the
whole jar with honey.

But suddenly something stung him. Then
something stung him again. Before he knew it,
he was covered with bee stings. They really hurt!

Rabbit had tricked him again!

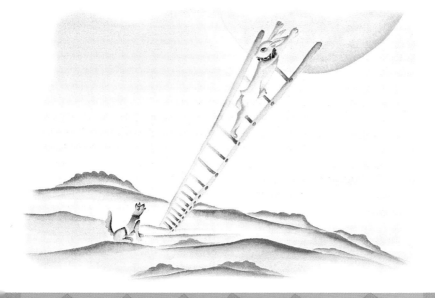

Rabbit was a smart fellow. He knew Coyote would never forgive him now. He knew he had to go far, far away from Coyote.

Luckily, deep in the hills was a ladder that reached the moon. The world's greatest engineer must have built that ladder. Rabbit knew just where the ladder was. Up the ladder he hopped. It took him almost all night to get to the moon.

From way up there, he looked down. There was Coyote, still hunting for him. Rabbit laughed. Coyote heard him and looked up. When he saw Rabbit, he howled with anger. He began looking for a way to get to the moon.

To this day, Coyote roams the hills, looking. And to this day, Rabbit sits up there on the moon, laughing.

Will Coyote ever find the ladder? *¿Quién sabe?* Who knows? Maybe, maybe not. If he does, watch out, Rabbit!

Until then, Coyote will never stop roaming the hills and howling at Rabbit up on the moon.